Steve & Wessley in

THE ICE CREAM SHOP

FOR
ROBIN
Ice Cream Aficionado

ISBN 978-0-545-61481-8

Copyright © 2014 by Jennifer E. Morris

All rights reserved. Published by Scholastic Inc.
SCHOLASTIC and associated logos are trademarks and/or registered trademarks of Scholastic Inc.

12 11 10 9 8 7 6 5 4 3 2 1   14 15 16 17 18 19/0

Printed in the U.S.A.   40
First printing, May 2014

Book design by Maria Mercado

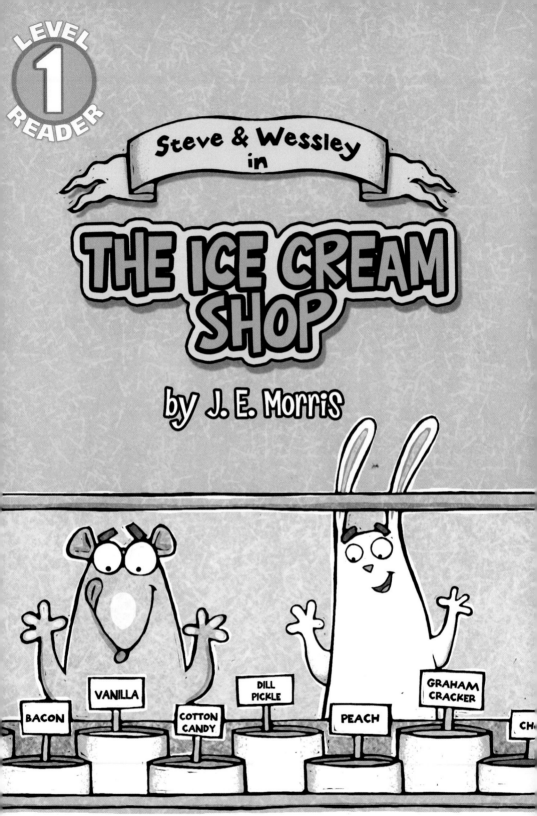

SCHOLASTIC INC.

Steve walked down the street.

Steve walked by an ice cream shop.

Steve liked ice cream.

Steve liked ice cream very much.

Steve pushed on the door.

Steve pushed again.

And again.

The door did not open.

Was the shop closed?
No, it was open.

Steve pushed on the door harder.

But the door still did not open.

Steve's tummy growled loudly.

Wessley walked down the street.

Wessley PULLED the door open.

Steve pulled the door open, too.

Steve and Wessley ordered their favorite flavors.

Steve and Wessley ate their
ice cream together.

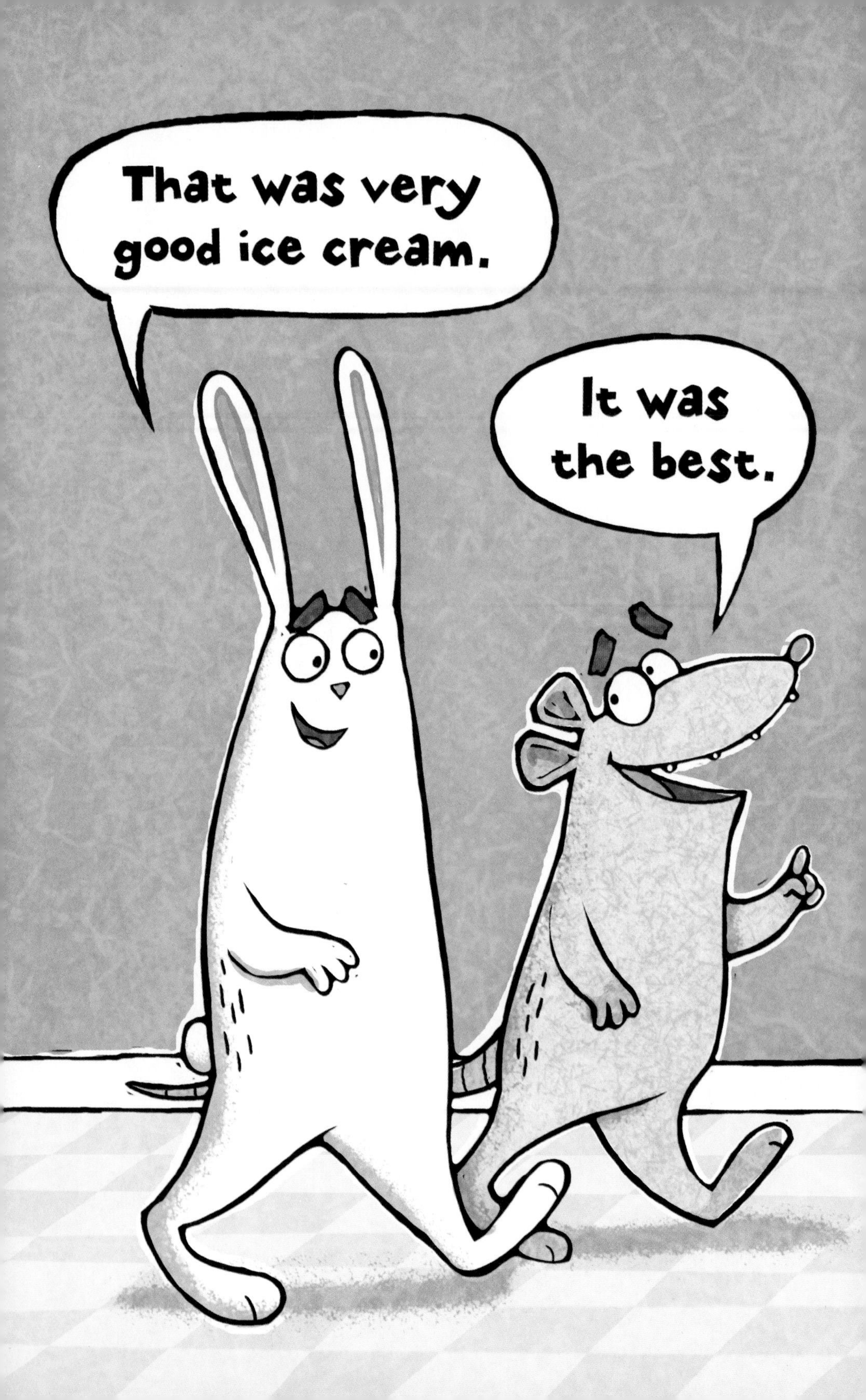
That was very good ice cream.
It was the best.

Now it was time for Steve
and Wessley to leave.